D0427368

DRAGONBREATH
THE CASE OF THE TOXIC MUTANTS

DRAGONBREATH
THE CASE OF THE TOXIC MUTANTS

BY
URSULA VERNON

DIAL BOOKS

an imprint of Penguin Group (USA) Inc.

For my grandmother, who paid for my dental work, a fact that I did not appreciate nearly enough at the time.

DIAL BOOKS
An imprint of Penguin Group (USA) Inc. • Published by the Penguin Group
Penguin Group (USA) Inc., 375 Hudson Street, New York, NY 10014, U.S.A.

USA/Canada/UK/Ireland/Australia/New Zealand/India/South Africa/China
Penguin Books Ltd, Registered Offices: 80 Strand, London WC2R 0RL, England
For more information about the Penguin Group visit penguin.com

Library of Congress Cataloging-in-Publication Data
Vernon, Ursula.
The case of the toxic mutants / by Ursula Vernon.
    p. cm. — (Dragonbreath ; 9)
 Summary: Danny Dragonbreath and his friends try to help the senior reptiles of Sunny Acres find a lost item.
 ISBN 978-0-8037-3847-8 (hardcover)
 [1. Lost and found possessions—Fiction. 2. Stealing—Fiction. 3. Dragons—Fiction.
4. Mystery and detective stories.] I. Title.
PZ7.V5985Cas 2013
[Fic]—dc23
2012026079

Printed in the U.S.A.

10 9 8 7 6 5 4 3 2 1

Designed by Jennifer Kelly
Text set in Stempel Schneidler

ALWAYS LEARNING   PEARSON

IT WAS A GLORIOUS
LATE-SUMMER DAY.

THE DREADED VISIT

"What?" Danny Dragonbreath shook off the hazy dreams of lazy summer days, and managed to focus on his mother, who was blocking the sun. "I just visited Great-Granddad. He's fine. He hasn't seen a ninja in months. Suki's helping him grow tomatoes."

"Not your *great*-grandfather," said his mom. "Your grandfather. On your father's side. At the home."

OH. *THAT* GRANDDAD.

This was not the ideal activity for a summer afternoon.

Actually, Danny would have had a hard time coming up with a *less* thrilling activity for a summer afternoon. Going to the dentist, maybe. Shopping for school stuff.

Come to think of it, shopping for school stuff was kind of fun, as long as you avoided buying one of the folders with something humiliating on it. You could pick out pencils based on their properties as missile weapons. Certainly it was a lot more fun than visiting his paternal grandfather.

"He doesn't like me!" Danny said. "He calls me a whippersnapper and tells me that when he was my age, he was working two jobs and eating knights. I don't *want* to eat knights! Dragons don't even eat knights anymore! They're an endangered species or something!"

"Oh, I'm sure he likes you fine," said Danny's mother, in a tone that indicated that A) Danny was quite right and B) it didn't actually matter that he was right. "He's just old and set in his ways."

"I can be young and set in my ways," offered Danny. "Here, I'll lie in this hammock and when you try to get me to move, I'll complain."

VERY FUNNY.

YOU KNOW, IN MY DAY, WHEN WE HAD TO VISIT OUR GRANDDADS, IT WAS UPHILL BOTH WAYS, AND—

DON'T PUSH YOUR LUCK.

Danny sighed and rolled out of the hammock, which involved a queasy moment when he nearly ended up in the dirt. "Can I go tomorrow?"

"Oh, no," said his mother. "He's bored or lonely or . . . well, bored. He's called today twice already, claiming that people at the home are stealing his false teeth. Go keep him entertained for an hour or two."

"But Mooommm. . . ." Danny dragged his feet. "He doesn't *want* me to come over. The last time I visited him, he told me that he had some very important business to attend to and I should leave. And then he went to sleep. I don't think he *likes* kids!"

"Don't worry," said his mother grimly, "he doesn't like grown-ups either. Remember the Thanksgiving we tried to have him over, and

he moved without a for-
warding address?"
"But—"

"KID, EITHER YOU GET HIM TO STOP CALLING OR YOUR FATHER IS GOING TO BECOME CONVINCED THAT HE SHOULD COME LIVE WITH US. AND NOBODY WANTS THAT.

"But—"

"You two would have to share a room."

"Gotta go, Mom, bye!" Danny tore out of the yard.

"Thought that'd work," muttered Danny's mother under her breath.

SLIME MOLDS AND TURLINGSWARDS

Danny was halfway to the bus stop when he decided to make a detour and pick up his best friend, Wendell the iguana. He had no idea how you entertained an elderly and cantankerous dragon, but Wendell might. Wendell was good with adults. They thought he was intelligent and serious and polite. (This was all true, but Danny tried not to hold it against him.) If anybody would know how to keep his grandfather happy, it would be Wendell.

"Thure," said Wendell, closing the front door behind him. "Let'th go."

Danny paused. "You feeling okay?"

OH. YEAH.
IT'TH MY NEW RETAINER.
THEY JUTHT ADJUTHTED IT,
AND MY TEETH FEEL
ALL WEIRD.

"Oooh! Did they give you metal fangs and stuff?"

"No, it just feels like my teeth are all different lengths," said the iguana, enunciating very clearly. "And if I'm not careful, I lisp a little." He grimaced. "The dentist says I'll be used to it in a couple of days, but I have to wear it for a whole *year.*"

A WHOLE
YEAR? DUDE!

"I'm going to loothe it," said Wendell morosely. "I know I am. If I don't loothe it, Big Eddy will thteal it. How can I keep track of thomething for a whole year?"

"You'll do better than I would," said Danny. "I'd have lost it before I was out of the dentist's office."

They reached the bus stop. Wendell checked the schedule, did some math, and announced that the bus would arrive in fourteen minutes. Danny saw no reason to question this.

"We've got time to go get Chrithtiana," Wendell added. "If you want."

Normally Danny would have thought twice about spending an afternoon with Christiana, Nerd Queen Extraordinaire. She was a friend, sure, but not a very comfortable one, and she still didn't believe he was a *real* dragon. But anybody he could bring along to keep his grandfather entertained was fine by him.

SURE! WONDERFUL! CHRISTIANA'S A GREAT IDEA!

Wendell gave him a suspicious look. "Where are we going that you're acthually happy to have Chrithtiana along?"

"Sunny Acres Reptile Village," said Danny. "My grandfather thinks people have been stealing his false teeth."

"How old ith your grandfather?" asked Wendell.

"I dunno. Eleventy hundred years or something. He's the size of a house."

Wendell accepted this without comment. A great many reptiles kept growing more or less forever, and retirement homes tended to have very large doorways as a result.

"Ith he a dragon?"

"Yeah. Not like Great-Granddad Dragonbreath, though."

HE'S A WESTERN DRAGON, SO HE LOOKS SORT OF LIKE DAD, ONLY, Y'KNOW, HUGE.

Christiana answered her door on the first knock. "Are we going somewhere?"

"Sunny Acres Reptile Village," said Danny.

"That'll work."

"What'th the exthperiment?" asked Wendell.

"I'm teaching a slime mold to run a maze." She considered. "Well . . . *ooze* a maze."

"Slime molds are *real*?" asked Danny. "I thought they were just—y'know, monsters in video games."

"Yeah, they're fungus things that grow in mulch."

"What kind are you uthing?" asked Wendell.

"*Fuligo septica*. Dog vomit slime mold."

THE DOG VOMIT SLIME MOLD IS SO NAMED BECAUSE IT LOOKS EXACTLY LIKE A DOG THREW UP IN YOUR FLOWERBED.
IT'S HARMLESS, IT JUST LOOKS ICKY.

"They're capable of surprisingly complex behaviors," Christiana said. "I'm trying to teach one to navigate a maze."

"Yeah, good luck with that," said Danny, remembering the problem at hand. "You know anything about entertaining old people?"

IT DEPENDS ON THE OLD PERSON. ARE THEY INTERESTED IN SLIME-MOLD TRAINING?

"He's mostly interested in sleeping," said Danny. "And writing letters to the editor."

Christiana clicked her tongue at him disapprovingly. "Have some respect. We'll all be old someday too, you know." She considered. "Well, Wendell and I will. You'll probably die in some kind of freak bottle rocket accident before you're twenty."

THAT'S THE NICEST THING YOU'VE EVER SAID TO ME.

SIGH . . .

"Anyway," said Christiana, once the bus had arrived and they had gotten settled on it, "the point is that just 'cos somebody's old doesn't mean they're automatically grumpy and boring. Have an open mind!"

Danny rolled his eyes. "I didn't say that he's grumpy and boring because he's *old*. There are some old people I like very much. My great-grandfather Dragonbreath is totally the coolest! My grandfather Turlingsward, however, is grumpy and boring *because he's grumpy and boring.*"

There was a brief silence while Christiana and Wendell absorbed the important bits of this speech.

TURLINGSWARD?!

"Wow," said Wendell. "No wonder your family went with 'Dragonbreath.' Imagine being Danny Turlingthward."

"He still hasn't forgiven my dad for changing his name," said Danny. "He usually forgets Christmas, but when he remembers, he gives Dad monogrammed socks that say *Turlingsward*."

"Bet those are hard to re-gift," said Christiana.

"Anyway," said Danny, who felt they were getting badly off the topic, "the point is that Granddad is, like—like—"

HE'S LIKE A *PROFESSIONAL CURMUDGEON!*

"You could have told us this *before* we got on the bus," said Christiana, looking at her transfer sadly.

"Yeah, well." Danny folded his arms. "Mom said that he thinks somebody's been stealing his false teeth. So we probably just have to find them, listen to him talk about the young people today, and then get off his lawn."

"That doethn't thound tho bad," said Wendell.

Danny hoped that the iguana was right.

A DIABOLICAL DENTURE THIEF

Sunny Acres Reptile Village was big. Like, *really* big.

Since so many elderly reptiles were extremely large—a boa constrictor grandmother could be fourteen feet long, and required both space to sun herself and an apartment large enough to hold her collection of commemorative spoons—Sunny Acres consisted of dozens of individual cottages with big yards. Each yard had an enormous flat rock in the sunshine. Between the cottages were hedges of tall grass and trees. A creek ran through the middle of the property, and there were birds singing in the trees.

"Thith playthe ith bigger than the mall!" said Wendell, looking around. "Where'th your grand-dad live?"

"Over in the back, near the creek," said Danny. He waved to the elderly boa constrictor on the nearest rock. "Hi, Mrs. Scalinghurst! Remember me?"

Mrs. Scalinghurst waved her tail at him. "Why, if it isn't little Danny! How you've grown since last time! My, it took us ages to clean up all the wreckage after that . . ." She flicked her tongue thoughtfully. "I figured we'd see you out here, given all the commotion."

"Not that anyone believes that fire-breathing nonsense," said Mrs. Scalinghurst cheerfully. "I suspect your grandfather's getting a trifle . . . ssss . . . *fuzzy* in his old age. But the idea of setting that nice woman's home on fire! Dear me! If he doesn't stop, they'll kick him out of Sunny Acres, and then where will he be?"

"Living in my room," said Danny glumly.

"Fire-breathing . . ." scoffed Christiana. *"Seriously?"*

Danny debated whether to argue that his grandfather *wasn't* senile, he was just a real dragon, and real dragons breathed fire . . . or just to smile and nod and go make sure that "Real Dragon Breathes Fire on Neighbor" did not become a story on the nightly news.

"Um . . ."

"Dithcrethon ith the better part of valor," said Wendell under his breath. "Let'th go."

"Huh?"

"Dithcrethon . . . Dith . . . Oh, never mind." The iguana rolled his eyes. "Let'th jutht go deal with your grandfather."

Most of the cottages looked alike, so Danny might have had a hard time figuring out which cottage he was looking for. Fortunately—if embarrassingly—they heard Grandfather Turlingsward long before they saw him.

They peered around the end of the hedge. Danny almost didn't want to look.

Standing on top of his rock, wearing spectacles and waving a scaly fist in the air, Grandfather Turlingsward was yelling across the path at . . . nobody.

A closed door and an abandoned drink indicated that someone—possibly the rumored Miss Flicktongue—had left the front yard a few minutes earlier. The fact that she wasn't there, however, didn't slow Grandfather Turlingsward down. If anything, it made him madder.

"Sure, go ahead and hide! When I burn your house down, where are you going to hide then?"

The ancient
dragon focused his
eyes on Danny. "Oh.
It's *you*." He didn't sound
terribly excited. "Harold's
boy. Harold *Turlingsward's* boy.
Have you gotten a job yet?"

"I'm still in grade school," said Danny patiently. "We don't have jobs. Granddad, you can't stand around threatening to burn people's houses down."

"Hmmph!" Grandfather Turlingsward looked annoyed, but he did lie down on his rock and fold his arms. "I'll do whatever I have to do, if she doesn't give my dentures back!"

"Why would anybody take your denthureth?" asked Wendell.

The old dragon rolled his head to one side and peered at Wendell. "Who's this?"

"This is my buddy Wendell. And this is Christiana."

"It's a pleasure to meet you, sir," said Wendell, speaking very carefully so as not to lisp.

"Hi," said Christiana.

"Is *this* the crew that's supposed to get my dentures back?" asked Grandfather Turlingsward. "You'll need more than that. That old biddy Flicktongue is wily."

Danny and his friends exchanged glances. Apparently his grandfather wasn't interested in the niceties. That was fine with Danny.

"*Why* would she take your dentures?" Wendell repeated, a little more loudly.

"How should I know?" asked Grandfather Turlingsward. "You expect me to know what goes on in the diabolical mind of a denture thief?" He waved a hand. "Just get them back! Do you know what it's like not to have dentures? I've been eating oatmeal for three days! Do you know what that does to my bowels?"

PLEASE DON'T TELL ME ANY MORE, GRANDDDAD!

You could say a lot of things about Christiana Vanderpool. Danny had said a lot of those things, over the years. She was nerdy and brainy and objected to really weird things. She still didn't believe Danny was a real dragon, and after he and Wendell had even taken her into the Fairy Realm, she had convinced herself that she'd hallucinated the whole thing.

But when it came to tackling a problem logically . . . well, you really couldn't do better than Christiana.

ALL RIGHT. LET'S TAKE THIS FROM THE TOP.

"When did you first notice the dentures missing?" she asked.

Grandfather Turlingsward looked pleased. "Finally, somebody's taking this seriously! Well, young lady, they vanished three nights ago. I'd put them in the bucket by the nightstand to soak, like I do every night, and when I woke up, they were gone!"

"I see." Christiana clasped her hands behind her back. "If you did it every night, then a thief would know exactly where to look for the dentures, wouldn't they?"

"Yes!" said Grandfather Turlingsward. "You see? Miss Flicktongue would have known she could find my dentures there!" He glared across the street at the absent Miss Flicktongue.

"We haven't ruled out the possibility of other thieves yet," said Christiana firmly. "Was your door locked?"

NO.
I NEVER LOCK
'EM.

"Is there anything else you can tell us?" asked Christiana. "Anything suspicious?"

Grandfather Turlingsward thought about it. "The window was open," he said finally. "I mean, it's summer, so it's usually a little open, but it was pushed all the way open. I don't usually do that."

"So the thief may have gone through the window!" said Christiana triumphantly.

Danny listened to the crested lizard interrogate his grandfather. Something was bothering him. There was something that the old dragon hadn't mentioned . . .

"Granddad?"

"Eh?"

"What about your hoard? If somebody broke into the house to steal stuff, wouldn't they have taken something from your hoard?"

The old dragon narrowed his eyes and made a ferocious *hrrrumph!* sound. It sounded like a car backfiring on a distant street. "Never you mind about my hoard, boy. My hoard's safe and sound. I keep *that* door locked up tight."

Danny was a little disappointed. He'd been hoping for a look at it. A dragon as old as Grandfather Turlingsward surely must have accumulated an enormous hoard over the years. Danny was pretty sure he kept it in the back bedroom. The last time he'd come over, the door had been open, and he'd caught a glimpse of coins and glittering jewels before his Grandfather had shut the door and grumbled about looky-loos. (Whatever that meant.)

For Danny, who had so far managed to accumulate five rolls of quarters, fifteen arcade tokens, and a genuine cubic zirconia in his hoard, this was very inspiring.

"That is a good question, though," said Christiana, nodding to Danny. "Is anything else missing, Mr. Turlingsward?"

"Nothing!" said the old dragon. "Except the bag of peanuts off the counter, and that's nothing new. You can't keep peanuts around here. The nurses take them. They say they don't, but other-wise somebody's breaking into my house every three days and stealing peanuts, and that's just crazy talk."

OH, SURE, *THAT'S* CRAZY . . .

"I'll make a note," said Christiana. "Now, can you describe the missing item? Do you have a photo, maybe?"

"Oh, *yes*," huffed Grandfather Turlingsward. "I *routinely* take photos of my dentures. I have

Dentures at the Beach and *Still Life with False Teeth.* I'm thinking of having a one-man show at the Museum of Modern Art." He sneered at Christiana, revealing a vast expanse of pink gums.

Danny and Wendell snickered.

Danny was impressed. He'd never heard his grandfather apologize to anybody before. He'd once hit Danny with the front door and blamed him for lollygagging on the front step, even though Danny was pretty sure he had never lollygagged in his life.

"All right, then," said Christiana. "You've been very helpful. We'll see what we can find out. We'll start by checking around the outside of your house for clues."

"You do that," said Grandfather Turlingsward, closing his eyes. "I'll be right here if you need me."

And with that, the elderly dragon went to sleep, right in front of them.

ANIMAL TRACKTH

"Who put you in charge?" Danny asked Christiana as they walked around the back of the cottage. "He's *my* granddad."

"You wanna be in charge?" asked the crested lizard. "Fine. Lead the way. I just thought you wanted to get out of here as quickly as possible."

Danny gritted his teeth. Christiana was always so *bossy.* And assuming that she could solve the mystery faster than he could! Sheesh! Just because he couldn't do math problems at the speed of light didn't mean he was bad at mysteries!

"You think there really ith a denthure thief?" asked Wendell skeptically.

"I know, it sounds crazy. But I think there are some interesting clues here. The open window. The missing peanuts. The footprints that you are *just* about to trample, Danny Dragonbreath!"

Danny froze.

"That'th not a clue," said Wendell scornfully. "Thothe are *animal* trackth."

"So?" Christiana shot back. "Plenty of animals steal things! Magpies and crows steal shiny objects all the time."

"You think a *bird* stole my granddad's dentures?" asked Danny. "Seriously? As big as he is, those dentures have got to weigh like fifty pounds. It'd take a whole flock of birds." He paused, struck by the mental image.

"Laden African thwallowth," said Wendell, and giggled at nothing in particular.

"Okay, maybe not birds," Christiana allowed. "But there are still animal tracks in the dirt there."

"Huh," said Danny. In movies, great detectives always looked at suspicious tracks and said things like "I see that this could only have been left by a six-foot-tall lizard with a limp, who has recently been to New Jersey!"

Apparently this was something they taught you in detective school, because they just looked like animal tracks to Danny.

"They go up to the window," said Wendell, pointing. "Do you think that'th the bedroom window?"

The window was firmly closed now.

"It looks like there's more than one animal," said Danny.

"Or one that walked around a lot," said Christiana.

The tracks were in soft dirt around the base of the window, which had a few patchy weeds. It turned into mowed grass a few feet out from the wall, though, and then into the tall, unmown meadow five or six feet past that.

"If they walked on the grath, they didn't leave any trackth," said Wendell gloomily.

Danny agreed. Who knew that footprints would be so unhelpful?

"We still need to gather more information," said Christiana. "Let's talk to Miss Flicktongue."

They walked across the street to Miss Flicktongue's cottage. Danny felt unexpectedly nervous—if she was nice, he was probably going to have to apologize for his granddad, and if she was mean, she was probably going to yell at him *about* his granddad. Neither option was very appealing.

Wendell, untroubled by such concerns, rang the bell.

Miss Flicktongue was a large lizard, but nowhere near the size of Danny's grandfather. Her cottage was smaller too, and looked like a large house, not an airplane hangar.

"Oh, dear!" she said. "Are you selling candy bars to raise money? I'm afraid I can't buy any just now—I do love your candy bars, but my dentures, you see . . ."

"We're thorry to bother you, ma'am," began

Wendell, who was an expert at schmoozing with grown-ups. "But we—"

"What's happened to your dentures?" asked Christiana, who was an expert at cutting to the chase.

"Oh, it's just so embarrassing." Miss Flicktongue flapped her apron with her hands. "I'm afraid they've gone missing. I feel terribly absentminded, but I haven't been able to find them, and I really have looked everywhere. And that poor man across the street has been bellowing at me—"

Danny flushed.

YEAH, UM, ABOUT THAT . . .

She looked at him inquiringly. Danny squirmed. She looked so *nice*. "Err . . . that's my granddad. I'm really sorry. He's kinda mean. It's . . . err . . ."

"Oh, he's usually a dear," she assured him. "He's gruff, but that's just his way. I know that. But he gets so upset whenever anything unexpected happens. He's a creature of habit, you know. He doesn't like surprises."

Danny could not imagine not liking surprises. Surprises were awesome! Just yesterday he'd opened the suitcase he'd forgotten to unpack after summer camp and found something very surprising, and his mother had said something even more surprising when she saw it.

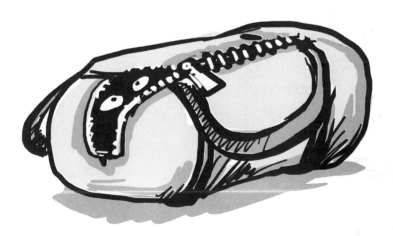

"When did you notice the dentures were missing?" asked Christiana, refusing to be distracted from the matter at hand.

"Just this morning," said Miss Flicktongue. "I usually keep them on my nightstand, you know, and when I went looking for them, they were gone!"

"Would you mind if we looked around?" Wendell asked. "We're invethtigating the crime."

"How clever of you!" said Miss Flicktongue. "Of course, please be my guests! I do so want my dentures back."

They tromped off the porch and around the side of the house. Much like Grandfather Turlingsward's cottage, there was a narrow side yard, surrounded by the tall hedge of unmown meadow. Unlike the other cottage, this one had a large flowerbed planted with flowers.

"More tracks!" Danny pointed.

"Thith ith more like it!" said Wendell happily. The broad flowerbed provided plenty of dirt for the animal tracks, and they were *everywhere*. They were clustered particularly tightly under the open window, as if something had walked back and forth under it.

"They come out of the tall grass," said Danny, following them back to where they emerged from the overgrown hedge.

"Makes sense," said Christiana. "It's where you'd expect animals to live."

"Unless somebody did break in," said Danny, "and they knew they wouldn't leave tracks in the grass, so they got back there as quickly as possible with the stolen dentures!"

Christiana did not seem impressed with this bit of deduction. "So how did they leave animal tracks instead of people tracks?"

"They could have strapped plaster casts of the animal tracks to their feet!" said Danny. "Then we'd *think* it was animals!"

"I don't have one yet," said Christiana. "We need more data." She turned back toward the front yard. "Let's see if Miss Flicktongue leaves that window open . . ."

Wendell followed. Danny gave one last look toward the tall grass, and froze.

Something was looking back.

THE VANISHING MISTER HONKERS

It was brown. Danny couldn't make out very many details—was it wearing a coat? Did it have some kind of long fur? It was only about two feet tall, and rather plump.

When it saw him, it let out a squeak and vanished. Danny almost went after the creature, but it moved too quickly.

He rushed after Wendell and Christiana, and found them talking to Miss Flicktongue.

GUYS! GUYS!
I SAW A THING! IT'S A THING!
THERE'S A THING!

I'M GONNA
NEED A MORE SPECIFIC
NOUN, DUDE.

IT WAS SORT OF BROWN AND FURRY AND SHORT . . .

IT COULD HAVE BEEN A WOODCHUCK.

OR A RARE PANAMANIAN PIRANHA RAT!

Danny would have been quite interested to hear more about the Panamanian piranha rat— did they swarm like piranhas? Could they skeletonize a cow in five minutes?—but Miss Flicktongue was talking.

61

ACCIDENTALLY CREATED WHEN AN AFRICANIZED RAT QUEEN ESCAPED CAPTIVITY, TAKING A SWARM OF NATIVE PIRANHA RATS WITH HER, THE PANAMANIAN PIRANHA RAT HAS BEEN SPREADING SLOWLY NORTH, TAKING OVER CANALS AND WATERWAYS. VICTIMS REPORT DOZENS OF TINY SNORKELS APPROACHING BEFORE THE ATTACK.

"We do get woodchucks around here," she said.

"I suppose it could have been a woodchuck . . ." said Danny dubiously. He wasn't entirely sure what a woodchuck looked like—most of what he knew about woodchucks involved how much wood they could chuck, if indeed they chucked wood at all—but he didn't think they usually wore coats. Wearing coats was very odd behavior. Danny had known several very intelligent rats, and even *they* didn't wear clothes.

"It looked like it was wearing something with a hood," he said slowly. "Sort of reddish."

"Woodchucks don't wear clothes," said Christiana. "Are you sure it wasn't a person?"

"It'd be a really tiny person," said Danny.

"Maybe it had an odd fur pattern," said Wendell. "Thome of them get mange, you know. If you thaw it thitting up . . ."

Danny shrugged. He hadn't gotten that good a look at it. Sometimes your eyes played tricks on you. He remembered one night when he'd seen an incredibly realistic monster in his bedroom, and when he screamed "DIE MONSTER SCUM!" and threw his clock radio at it, it turned out to be a pile of laundry, a lamp, and a rubber chicken.

His mother had been very sarcastic about it.

"Excuse me one moment," said Miss Flick-tongue, and bustled into the house. From across the street, Grandfather Turlingsward opened one eye and glared at them. "Probably going to destroy evidence," he grumbled, in a whisper that could be heard a block away.

"Maybe she needs to use the restroom," said Christiana practically.

"I don't think she took your dentures, Grand-dad," said Danny. "For one thing, hers are missing too."

"The times don't match," said Christiana. "Hers have been gone for one day, and yours have been gone for three. And also . . . err . . ."

I'M SAYING SHE COULDN'T USE YOUR DENTURES, EXCEPT MAYBE AS A FOOTSTOOL.

"Hmmph!" Grandfather Turlingsward dropped his chin back onto the warm rock and glared across the street. "Maybe she stole them for some other nefarious purpose, then. Look at all those flowers! I bet she planted petunias in them!"

Danny was forced to admit that this was the most plausible theory yet. Miss Flicktongue was apparently one of those people who thought it was cute to grow plants in watering cans, old boots, little red wagons, and various other junk. There were even plants growing in a pair of high heels on the porch.

Could the missing dentures be lurking somewhere, disguised with geraniums? He lifted the
leaves of a particularly dense fern, to reveal . . .
"Whoa," said Wendell. "It'th in a toilet!"

"Country kitsch," said Christiana grimly. "Mark my words, somewhere around here, there's a stone goose that she dresses up for holidays."

"You mean Mister Honkers?" asked Miss Flicktongue, emerging from the house. "Oh, I miss him! He went missing a few months ago. I thought it was just kids—no offense meant, my dears, I mean *bad* children—but now that my dentures are gone, I wonder . . ." She sighed. "And he was wearing the most adorable little outfit too."

Christiana swung around and gazed vaguely into the distance, with the air of one who is resisting saying "I told you so," with great effort.

"It doesn't seem like Mister Honkers can be related, though," said Miss Flicktongue, pursing her lips. "Somebody really didn't like him. I used to make him the most darling little outfits, and they were always vanishing, especially at Christmas. Some people have no holiday spirit!"

A loud snort came from the rock across the street.

Danny thought that the prime suspect was probably pretending to sleep about twenty feet away, but this was the Case of the Missing Dentures, not the Case of the Vanishing Goose.

WOULD YOU CHILDREN LIKE SOME COOKIES AND LEMONADE YOU HAVE TO KEEP YOUR STRENGTH UP WHILE INVESTIGATING!

"It's been twenty minutes," Christiana said. "We aren't—"

Wendell elbowed her in the ribs. The iguana did not get cookies at home, unless they were made with carob and brown rice. "We'd love some," he said, making an effort to speak clearly around his retainer. "It's very nice of you to offer."

The cookies were chocolate chip, and very good. "I freeze the dough in batches," explained

Miss Flicktongue, "for when my little nieces and nephews come over. I do love how baking cookies make a house smell, don't you?"

. . . ADOPT ME?

"Well," said Christiana, licking the last crumbs off her fingers. "I think we've got a few interesting points to consider."

Danny rolled his eyes. There went Christiana, taking over again.

She noticed the eye-roll. "*You* want to sum up, Danny?"

"Sure!" Danny began ticking points off. "First

of all, more than one set of dentures is missing. Second, Granddad's dentures went missing first. Third, there's animal tracks all over the ground outside the windows. Fourth, I saw a weird animal. Fifth . . . err . . . fifth . . ."

"Fifth," said Wendell, holding up a finger, "other thtuff hath gone mithing. The peanuth, and Mithter Honkerth."

"Does that stuff matter?" asked Danny. "I mean, they might not be related at all."

"We don't know yet what's relevant and what isn't," said Christiana, nodding to Wendell.

WE HAVE TO KEEP AN OPEN MIND.

Danny snorted. She was one to talk. Christiana's mind, on the subject of dragons, was closed tighter than a steel bear trap.

"I don't know about you guys," said Christiana, "but I think we need to do some research."

"I concur," said Wendell.

Danny sighed. It was always the same with Wendell and Christiana. Take them on a thrilling adventure, and they *always* wanted to stop at the library.

Still, if the alternative was hanging around with his grandfather . . .

He slid off the rock. "Okay. You guys tell Miss Flicktongue, and I'll go explain to Granddad . . ."

"I saw you over there," grumbled Grandfather Turlingsward, opening one eye. "Fraternizing with the enemy, that's what it was. Hmmph!" The old dragon shot twin jets of smoke out of his nostrils. Danny looked around hurriedly for Christiana, but she had her back turned and was talking to Miss Flicktongue. Darn.

I DON'T THINK COOKIES AND LEMONADE COUNT AS FRATER . . . FRAT . . . WHATEVER YOU SAID.

"We're going to the library," said Danny. "My friends—Wendell and Christiana, you met them—they're really smart. They think they might be able to figure out what's stealing your dentures."

"I know what's stealing my dentures, and it's a who, not a what!" snapped Grandfather Turlingsward. He grumbled for a moment. "Still . . . if they're researching the workings of the criminal mind . . ."

"Criminal mind," said Danny. "Absolutely. Wendell was talking all about it. Said he just needed to check a few books."

"Hmmph!" said Grandfather Turlingsward, but he looked grudgingly impressed. "All right. Get to the library, then, and don't come back until you're willing to arrest the denture thief!"

"I don't think we can really arrest people . . ." said Wendell apologetically.

"Citizen's arrest!" roared Grandfather Turlingsward. "That's the problem with you young people! No drive! No gumption! No willingness to stand up to wrong-doers!"

"I think I hear the bus," said Danny. (This was absolutely not true, but the dragon felt it was a lie in the service of a good cause.) He and Wendell hurried toward the bus stop, pausing only to pick up Christiana on the way.

They were halfway down the block when Danny glanced behind him.

"Hey! Watch where you're going!" said Wendell as Danny stepped on his foot.

"Oh!" Danny turned back. "Sorry, dude . . ."

He could have sworn that when he looked back, just for a moment, he'd seen another of those little furry figures.

It had whisked out of sight so quickly, Danny hadn't been able to make out any details. But just for a second, he'd had the impression—well, it was pretty crazy, but he could have sworn that the figure was wearing a tiny yellow rain slicker.

"Nah," he said to himself. "That's just nuts."

Still, he wondered . . .

A TRAGIC LOSS

The Slithering Heights public library was a big, comfortable building with lots of posters that told people to "Find Adventure in a Book!" Danny had fond memories of the kids' section, but of course Wendell and Christiana headed for the shelves where the books had no illustrations and very small type.

The card catalog had been put on computers recently, and so both the iguana and the crested lizard pulled up keyboards and began typing. They conferred together quietly, a conversation about decimal numbers and cross references that quickly excluded Danny.

"So . . ." he said.

"Leave this to us," said Christiana. "We'll get it done quicker."

The dragon felt annoyed. He could do research *too*. He'd researched a whole paper on volcanoes last spring, with a bibliography and everything. It was a solid C+ paper! Maybe even a B, if he hadn't drawn the sacrifices being thrown to the volcano god. His teacher hadn't appreciated that nearly enough.

It would serve them right if he found the critical bit of information that blew this case wide open.

He picked a computer terminal away from the other two and stared at the screen.

What if it wasn't some kind of normal animal? What if the explanation was something more mythical? Danny was great at mythical stuff.

What sort of mythical creature would steal dentures?

What if it didn't mean to steal dentures?

WHAT
IF IT'S REALLY
AFTER *TEETH?*

Lots of mythical creatures weren't very bright. Maybe they couldn't tell the difference between dentures and teeth. If you were a mythical creature out hunting for loose teeth, and you came across Grandfather Turlingsward's dentures, wouldn't that seem like you'd hit the mother lode of teeth?

"You guys!" cried Danny, standing up from the keyboard. "I've got it!"

IT'S AN EVIL TOOTH FAIRY!

"Your parents probably should have told you this already," said Christiana, "but Danny, there is no Tooth Fairy."

"There are totally fairies," said Danny.

"Oh. Hmm." Danny thought about that. If it really was a Tooth Fairy, then yeah, it would have to leave payment for the teeth it took. Given the size of Grandfather Turlingsward's dentures, a couple of gold bars might even be in order.

"Anyway, I don't think we should—" Wendell began.

"You're not lisping," said Christiana. "Wendell, where's your retainer?"

MY RETAINER!

"Oh god, I've lost it," moaned the iguana. "It's gone. My mom is going to have to get me a new one. She'll die. It's really expensive. Maybe I should run away from home."

"You could join the circus!" said Danny. "And change your name and become a lion tamer and—"

"Where did you have it last?" asked Christiana.

"—and teach them to jump through hoops and—"

"I took it out when we were eating cookies at Miss Flicktongue's. I bet I left it on the big rock out front."

"—you could even have a bullwhip!" said Danny.

"Many circuses are very cruel to the animals in them," said Christiana disapprovingly.

"I'd be very nice to the lions," said Wendell, "so they don't turn on me." He considered for a moment. "Does it *have* to be lions? Couldn't I tame, like, butterflies?"

"Or, y'know, we could just go back there and find your retainer," said Christiana.

Wendell relaxed a bit. "You think it's still there?"

"Unless the denture thief took it," said Christiana, turning back to her computer.

Wendell made a noise like somebody had stepped on his tail.

OH, NO . . .

"That just means we have to solve the mystery!" said Danny, and dove back into the computer files.

Half an hour later, all three kids gathered by the reference desk with their books.

"Book on animal track identification," said Christiana, holding up one of her choices. "I'm pretty sure I know what it is, but I want to identify it in the field to be sure. What about you guys?"

"I was too busy worrying about my retainer," said Wendell gloomily. He clutched *Butterfly Taming for Fun and Profit* closer to his chest.

"The astonishing thing isn't that you found that book," said Christiana, eyeing it, "it's really that it ever got written at all." She glanced over at Danny.

"Great Detectives Through the Ages!" said Danny, holding up one of his books. He'd spent the last ten minutes paging through the book, and while parts of it were pretty boring, there was some really interesting stuff about dead bodies. "Did you know that in 1248, there was a Chinese book called *The Washing Away of Wrongs* that told people how to tell the difference between drowning and strangling? Isn't that cool?"

". . . actually, I knew that," murmured Wendell.

"And listen to this! A guy named Thomas Bell discovered that if people are drowned or hanged, their teeth turn pink after they die! Pink teeth!" Danny waved his arms.

ISN'T THAT GROSS AND AWESOME!?

YES, BUT IT'S NOT RELEVANT. NOBODY'S DEAD.

I WILL BE WHEN I TELL MY MOM I'VE ALREADY LOST MY RETAINER.

"Fine," muttered Danny, "but I'm checking this book out anyway, in case any dead bodies show up."

"If any dead bodies show up, we're calling the police," said Christiana.

"Butterfly training, step one," read Wendell. "Get a very, very tiny chair . . ."

"What's your other book?" asked Christiana.

Danny set aside *Great Detectives Through the Ages* and revealed his second book with a flourish.

"*Aztec Myths and Legends?*" Christiana frowned. "It was a pretty impressive empire in its day, I grant you, but what do *Aztecs* have to do with your grandfather's dentures?"

"Step two," Wendell murmured, "select a cocoon . . ."

"I think it's an ahuizotl!" said Danny.

Wendell looked up from his book. Christiana blinked.

A-HOO-A-WHAT?

Danny was enormously pleased to have found a creature that Christiana had never heard of. He'd had to practice pronouncing the name under his breath, but it was worth it. "An ahuizotl! It's an Aztec monster. It's like a mutant otter with a hand on the end of its tail—*and it steals teeth!*"

He consulted the relevant section of the book. "It drowns people and takes their teeth. Also their eyeballs and their fingernails, but I guess that doesn't really apply—"

"*Nobody is missing their eyeballs,*" said Christiana. "But *you* must be missing your marbles!"

"I'm telling you, it makes sense!" said Danny. "The ahuizotl comes out of the creek, leaves all those tracks, goes in through the window, steals the teeth—"

"Wouldn't it have to drown your granddad first?" asked Wendell. "I mean, what I've read about ahuizotls says that they only take teeth and fingernails from their victims."

DUDE. CAN YOU IMAGINE AN OTTER TRYING TO DROWN MY GRANDDAD?

"You'd need an Olympic swimming pool," said Christiana. "Actually—wait, what am I saying? This is ridiculous! It's not an Aztec monster! How would an Aztec monster, even if such a thing existed, get here from Mexico?"

"It could stow away in a box of fruit," said Wendell. "Or on the landing gear of a plane. That's how the Guam tree snake got everywhere." For Danny's benefit he said, "They're little tiny snakes. Not like people-snakes."

"I am *familiar* with the Guam tree snake," said Christiana grimly. "Guam tree snakes are not mutant Aztec teeth-stealing otters!"

"I did see a little brown creature," said Danny. "That could have been the ahuizotl!"

"No, it couldn't have, *because ahuizotls don't exist!*"

YOU JUST DON'T WANT TO BELIEVE IN ANYTHING MYTHICAL!

"Maybe we should go outside," said Danny.
"Maybe we should get my retainer," said Wendell.
Christiana stalked off, her tail quivering with rage.

THE MUTANTS ARE COMING!

The ride back to Sunny Acres was not an entirely pleasant one. Christiana was ignoring Danny, and Wendell was immersed in his guide to butterfly taming.

IT SAYS HERE THAT THE TIGER SWALLOWTAIL IS PARTICULARLY FEROCIOUS!

Danny amused himself by reading more *Great Detectives Through the Ages*. The style was a bit dry and there were no pictures, but it was full of murders and blood and mysteries.

They were most of the way back to Sunny Acres when Danny judged that Christiana had probably cooled off. She got mad at him all the time, but she didn't stay mad for long, which was good. It would have been difficult to be friends otherwise.

"So what do *you* think it is?" he asked, leaning over the seat.

Christiana gave him a look, then apparently decided to forgive him. "I don't know yet. I'll need to look at the tracks to be sure."

"Sunny Acres!" called the bus driver, and they all piled off the bus again.

Mrs. Scalinghurst was still out on her rock. She smiled at them. "So busy today! My goodness!"

"Gotta run," said Danny, waving.

"All right. You children be careful playing back there—the old hospital building used to be behind those cottages, and heaven knows what's still out there . . . scalpels or needles or X-ray machines, I don't know what all."

Danny immediately vowed to return and find a broken X-ray machine as soon as possible.

They rounded the corner, and Wendell ran down the sidewalk to the rock in the front yard, scanning for his retainer. "I was sitting here—so it should be right here—or maybe here—"

IT'S GONE . . .

"The thief must have gotten it," said Christiana.

"What am I going to tell my mom?" asked Wendell hopelessly.

"We'll get it back," Danny said. "We'll catch the denture thief, Wendell, don't worry."

Across the street, Grand-
father Turlingsward was still on his rock. Danny
thought that he was really asleep this time. Every
few minutes he'd let out a snore and the windows
in Miss Flicktongue's cottage would rattle a little.

"I guess we could ask if he saw anything," said Christiana.

"Let's not wake him up," said Danny. *"Please."* He didn't think he could handle another session with his grandfather, so soon after the last one.

"Let's check the tracks," said Christiana, opening one of her books.

Danny and Wendell crowded around as the crested lizard opened to the page on pack rats.

They looked at the tracks.

They looked at the book.

They looked at the tracks again.

"Aha!" said Christiana. She brandished the book. "As I suspected! It's a pack rat!"

"Pack rat?" Danny frowned. "Is that like a rat that carries a little pack around, or rats that run in packs, like wolves?"

"It's a type of wood rat," said Christiana. "Not

like a *rat*-rat. They
collect stuff. Particularly
shiny objects. I think one
found the dentures and
wanted them for its nest."

"Sometimes they climb up
into the engines of cars and
chew on the wires," said Wendell, putting down
his butterfly book. "And they can build these
huge nests called middens. They're full of sticks
and twigs and any neat stuff the pack rat found
to drag home."

Christiana nodded.

"Maybe ahuizotl tracks look like pack rat
tracks?" asked Danny hopefully.

"It's an aquatic monster," said Christiana.
"They'd be webbed."

It wasn't that Danny *minded* when Christiana
was right, he just wished she wouldn't do it so
often, and in that tone of voice.

There was no denying that pack rats were possible . . . but so were ahuizotls, right? Just because

Christiana didn't believe in them didn't mean they weren't out there!

On the other hand, he had to admit that it would probably be easier to get the dentures back from a pack rat than from a monster that drowned people and stole their eyeballs. Hmm.

THAT IS A PROBLEM . . .

". . . hang on a minute," said Wendell, staring at the dirt.

"They're identical," said Christiana. "Those are totally pack rat tracks."

"Can I see the book?"

Christiana handed over the book. Wendell examined the drawing of the tracks, and then the tracks themselves.

"They look like pack rat tracks," the iguana admitted. "They're the right shape. But did you look at the scale?"

Christiana looked surprised. "No, I guess I didn't. Why?"

"The biggest pack rat in North America is twenty inches long," said Wendell, "and most of that is tail. And they have tiny little feet. Those tracks are at least six inches long. In order to leave a track that size, how big would the pack rat have to *be*?"

Danny almost never saw Christiana at a loss, but he was seeing it now. She took the book, looked at the text, looked at the tracks, and said "Huh!"

PACK RAT

"Could it be a giant pack rat?" asked Danny. "Like a giant mutant pack rat! Maybe it ate some radioactive seeds and it grew enormous and pretty soon it'll go rampage through the city—"

He was sad to abandon the ahuizotl theory, but if it involved a giant mutant pack rat, that was pretty cool too.

"There's a couple of them," said Wendell. "At least three distinct individuals. This one's got a crooked hind toe, and one of them is missing a claw on the front feet."

"Jeez," said Danny. "Listen to you, Daniel Boone! Get your mom to buy you a coonskin cap."

They trekked back to the front yard thoughtfully. Danny went to sit down on the rock, and then jumped up again. "Hey, Wendell—is this where your retainer was?"

"Did you find it?" asked the iguana excitedly.

"No—but this was sitting here." He held out a bedraggled hunk of fabric with a puff on the end. "I think it's a clue!"

"That's not a clue, that's a *Santa hat*," said Christiana. "A little tiny one."

"Something took my retainer and left a Santa hat," said Wendell. "Oh, Mom is going to be *thrilled*."

"That's consistent with a pack rat," Christiana admitted. "They frequently drop what they're carrying to pick up something new—but what was it doing with a Santa hat?"

"Christmas isn't for months," said Danny.

THE MYSTERY DEEPENS!

"The only thing deepening is the trouble I'm going to be in," muttered Wendell.

"Oh, you're back!" said Miss Flicktongue, opening the screen door. "Have you had any luck, children?"

"We've found a clue!" said Danny happily. "Do you recognize this object?" He waved the Santa hat at her.

"Oh my!" Miss Flicktongue lifted up her glasses to inspect the hat. "Oh dear me, yes! This is mine!"

I HAVEN'T SEEN THIS FOR AGES.

MISTER HONKERS WAS WEARING IT LAST CHRISTMAS, BUT SOMEBODY STOLE HIS LITTLE OUTFIT. AND IT TOOK ME FOREVER TO SEW IT TOO!

"And we found it in her yard too," muttered Christiana. "Astonishing!"

Danny ignored her. She was just jealous because *he'd* found the clue.

"A pack rat *could* have taken the outfit," said Christiana thoughtfully.

"Oh!" said Miss Flicktongue. "I always thought—well—" She dropped her voice to a whisper. "I'm sorry, young man, but I always thought that your grandfather took it! He never had a kind word to say about Mister Honkers."

SO THAT MEANS . . . IT WAS **WEARING** THE SANTA SUIT!

"What?" said Wendell.

Christiana rolled her eyes.

"The thing I saw!" Danny waved his arms. "It was really filthy, so I didn't recognize it, because it wasn't red anymore, but I think it was wearing a Santa outfit! And it was wearing the hat, so it must have taken the retainer and left the hat behind!"

He turned. "Miss Flicktongue—ma'am—this is really important! Did your goose have a little yellow raincoat too?"

"Oh, yes," said Miss Flicktongue. "He was wearing it when he vanished." She sniffled. "Poor Mister Honkers!"

THE PACK RATS ARE STEALING MISTER HONKERS'S CLOTHES!

A brief silence followed this pronouncement.

"Right," said Christiana. "I gotta sit down."

"But they actually stole Mister Honkers," said Wendell. "Like, the whole goose."

"Well, they probably aren't very bright," said Danny.

Wendell rubbed his forehead and sighed. "Let's move on. Okay. Assume that these are—I dunno, some kind of giant pack rats—and they've stolen dentures and my retainer and Miss Flicktongue's goose. Somewhere, there's probably a stash with all our stuff in it."

BUT HOW DO WE FIND THE MIDDEN—YOU KNOW, THE PACK RAT NEST? THERE'S ACRES AND ACRES HERE TO SEARCH.

DON'T WORRY, I HAVE A PLAN!

I CAN HARDLY WAIT . . .

OPERATION DENTURE/RETAINER

"It's all right here in this book," said Danny, waving *Great Detectives Through the Ages.* "When you think you've got your criminal, but you have to catch him in the act. We need a sting operation!"

"Eh?" said Wendell, who had been busy mourning his retainer. "What? I'm allergic to stings. I swell up and can't breathe and die. It's kind of a problem."

NOT THAT KIND OF STING. WE NEED TO FOLLOW THE PACK RATS BACK TO THEIR DEN. AND THAT MEANS WE'RE GONNA NEED BAIT.

"No," said Grandfather Turlingsward. "Absolutely not. No, no, a thousand times no. You're not touching my hoard."

"But Granddad!" said Danny. "We need something shiny! It doesn't have to be valuable! And we'll give it back as soon as we've tracked the pack rats."

"Pack rats!" His grandfather blew a puff of smoke through his nostrils. "I don't know where you got this fool notion about pack rats in your head! Anybody can see it's that harpy across the street!"

"If it's not pack rats, then nothing will happen to whatever you loan us," said Wendell patiently. "This is just to test our hypothesis."

"Not gonna happen, young whippersnapper!"

"Fine!" said Danny, exasperated. "Don't help us! Eat oatmeal forever! If we *do* get your dentures back, I'm gonna sell them on the Internet!"

"I'm sure Miss Flicktongue will loan us something," said Wendell. "She's been *very* nice about all this."

"Unlike *some* people," said Christiana.

Danny was so annoyed with his grandfather that he turned on his heel and stomped across the street. He was nearly to the other curb when Grandfather Turlingsward said, "Hold your horses, boy."

Turlingsward heaved a sigh like an earthquake. "All right . . . all right . . . I'm sure I've got something . . ."

He got up from his rock and lumbered into the cottage.

Ten minutes later, Grandfather Turlingsward returned, carrying a small piece of jewelry. It was a brooch set with dozens of sparkling gems that glittered in the sunlight.

"Wow!" said Wendell. "Are those diamonds?"

"Cubic zirconium," said Danny, who, like all dragons, knew exactly how much any object in a hoard was worth. He turned the brooch in his hands. "The setting's pewter. Workmanship's not bad, though. I'd say . . . sixty, seventy dollars."

"Ha!" said his grandfather, and patted him on the head. Since Grandfather Turlingsward's claws were as big as Danny, the smaller dragon had to brace himself to avoid being knocked flat. "I may have misjudged you, boy. You're a dragon to your tail-tip."

Danny wasn't quite willing to forgive his granddad for being so grumpy all the time, but he had to admit that the old dragon's praise felt good. He mumbled a thank-you.

Christiana started to say something—Danny caught the words *mass delusions*—and he hastily interrupted. "Is it shiny enough?"

"That? It should be shiny enough for a dozen pack rats. What's the next stage in your plan, Danny?"

Danny grinned. "We bait the trap. Then we hide!"

YOU HAVE
TO HIDE TOO,
GRANDDAD.

SURE.
GO GET A BUS
AND I'LL BE HAPPY TO
LIE DOWN BEHIND
IT.

MAYBE
YOU COULD GO
INSIDE?

Danny placed the brooch on the rock in Miss Flicktongue's front yard. It threw little bits of light across the lawn.

It was clear that Grandfather Turlingsward didn't

want to leave even a tiny part of his hoard unat-
tended, but he grumped and grumbled and finally
went inside his cottage. Danny could see him
watching through the window.

He hoped that he was right about being able to get the brooch back. Seventy dollars was a *lot* of chore money.

I'D HAVE TO WASH THE CAR . . . THE OTHER CAR . . . THE WINDOWS . . . THE HOUSE . . . THE LAWN . . .

He wasn't even sure *how* you washed a lawn.

Danny, Christiana, and Wendell hunkered down behind the various potted plants in Miss Flicktongue's garden. Wendell crouched down behind a planter, and Christiana hid behind a fern. Danny was the closest to the rock, behind a bathtub full of petunias.

They waited.

After a few minutes, Wendell leaned out from behind the planter and whispered, "Are you sure about this?"

"Completely sure!" Danny hissed. "Stay quiet!"
They waited some more.

Danny was beginning to wonder if they'd been wrong. Maybe Christiana had misidentified the tracks, and it wasn't pack rats after all. Maybe he'd been wrong, and they weren't going to take the bait.

Even if the weird little figures in Mister Honkers's clothes weren't pack rats, though, they should still go for the bait, right? Whatever they were, they were definitely stealing stuff.

Surely the brooch was more interesting to a pack rat than Wendell's retainer! You'd have to be really desperate to think Wendell's retainer was cool.

But wait—what was that, peering over the top of the rock?

It was the pack rat!

Danny wanted to cheer, but that would just have scared it off again. He twisted his tail between his hands. If it'd just get a little closer . . .

The pack rat climbed on top of the rock. It was wearing Mister Honkers's little yellow rain slicker and hat. It had a long snout and long furry tail.

Now that it was closer, Danny could see that the rain slicker didn't fit it terribly well. It had rolled the sleeves up over its paws, like a kid wearing pants that were too long for him. The hem looked as if it had been gnawed short to fit.

It was also much larger than the sewer rats Danny had met during that whole crazy episode with the potato salad and the were-wieners. Sewer rats were supposed to be huge, weren't they? You heard about them all the time. The alligators who worked in sewers in New York were always talking about how the sewer rats were as big as bison and ate subway passengers.

Regardless, the pack rat was still the largest rat Danny had ever seen. It was a good two feet high, and when you started thinking about it as a big rodent instead of a little tiny person, it didn't take much for your perspective to shift.

Would it take the bait?

The pack rat looked around one last time, its little pink nose working frantically—and then it snatched the brooch and took off running!

AFTER HIM!

The pack rat was weighed down by the brooch, and it was running on its hind legs, which probably wasn't easy for a rat, and it was wearing a raincoat originally made for a stone goose, which couldn't fit very well—and it was *still* incredibly fast!

Danny charged around the corner of Miss Flicktongue's cottage in time to see it dive into the tall grass. He dove after it. He wasn't going to lose sight of the pack rat now, not after his plan had worked!

The grass was hard to run through, but it couldn't be much easier for the pack rat. Danny followed the line of moving stalks, and caught occasional flashes of the yellow raincoat. He could hear Christiana behind him, and farther back, Wendell wheezing. The grass whipped against his arms as he ran.

Suddenly the grass vanished—and so did the ground!

Danny had to skid to a halt, and nearly fell off the edge of the embankment. The grass had led right up to the edge of the stream that ran through Sunny Acres. Fortunately it wasn't a very tall cliff—only a couple of feet down—and Danny was able to catch himself by clutching at clumps of grass growing along the water's edge.

He was just in time to see the pack rat's tail vanish into a hole in the opposite bank.

FWOOOP!

INTO THE MIDDEN . . .

"Guys! Guys!" yelled Danny. "Get over here! I found their lair!"

"Technically it'd be a den or a midden," said Christiana, coming up behind him. "*Lair* is more appropriate for carnivores."

"And supervillains and bat monsters," added Wendell.

"They might be carnivores," said Danny. "Or supervillains. I mean, we don't *know*, do we? They're already like giant mutant clothes-wearing pack rats. There could be meat in there. Or a death ray."

THINK WE CAN FIT?

OH, TOTALLY. PIECE OF CAKE.

JUST ONCE, I WOULD LIKE TO HAVE AN ADVENTURE THAT DOES NOT INVOLVE ME CRAWLING INTO A DARK HOLE IN THE GROUND!

"Ah, c'mon, Wendell . . . what's the worst that happens?" Danny got down on his hands and knees and peered into the hole. "They probably *don't* have a death ray."

"They could carry bubonic plague," said Wendell. "Lots of rodents do."

"Boo . . . Bub . . . ?"

BUBONIC PLAGUE! THE BLACK DEATH! YOU GET HORRIBLE PUS-FILLED LUMPS AND THEN THEY EXPLODE AND YOU DIE!

"Ooooh . . ." Danny was eager to go after the pack rat, but time spent talking about exploding pus was never wasted, as far as he was concerned.

"It's what we love about you, Wendell," said Christiana. "You're such an optimist."

"Fine! When you all have the Black Death, don't come crying to me!"

WELL, WE MAY HAVE THE BLACK DEATH, BUT YOU KNOW WHAT ELSE WE'LL HAVE?

WHAT?

. . . YOUR RETAINER.

. . . FINE.
LET'S GO.

Danny squared his shoulders and prepared to boldly go where no dragon had gone before.

The pack rat's midden was dark. Danny couldn't see anything. He wished he'd brought a flashlight, but it wasn't as if, when he'd gotten up this morning, he'd known that he was going to be chasing a mutant pack rat into a hole.

The ground was damp and squishy, probably because it was so close to the stream, and there were bits of roots dangling from the ceiling that kept scraping across his face. It felt like bugs. Danny would have hotly denied being scared, but he certainly didn't like it.

The tunnel twisted and turned too. He ran into a wall twice and had to feel along the sides with his hands to find out which way to go.

"Left!" he called back.

"Got it," said Christiana.

"I hate this so much," said Wendell. "I hate this like dental work. And family reunions."

Danny could make out a light up ahead in the tunnel. It wasn't very bright, but it was definitely there. When he flapped a hand in front of his face, he could see the motion.

He went around one more bend and the tunnel opened into a large room.

Danny stopped.

"What is it?" asked Christiana, coming up behind him.

"Is it plague?" called Wendell.

UH, GUYS . . .

SLIMY, SMELLY SLUDGE

Danny had been in a number of caverns in his time. There was some justice to Wendell's complaint. There had been the giant bat-cave in Mexico, the potato salad's lair in the sewers . . . that one weird cave that had been in Wendell's head . . .

Caves didn't bother him. He was a dragon, and dragons, while they mostly lived in nice houses and apartments these days, had historically been quite familiar with caves. Danny had no fear of being underground.

He had to admit, however, that this was a lot weirder than anything he'd expected to find under Sunny Acres.

Green slime oozed along the floor, dripping from a pipe on the far side of the room. It glowed faintly in the dark, providing an unhealthy half-light to the room. The pack rats had built up walls of junk on either side, making a kind of slime-canal through the room. The slime was crisscrossed by narrow bridges, and there was another, larger tunnel on the far side.

Danny moved to one side so that Christiana could crawl out. She looked around and said, "Huh!"

"Lotta pack rats," he said.

The iguana was right. There were at least a dozen pack rats, standing on the bridges and peering out of little dens made of sticks, and they were all looking at the intruders.

They didn't look mad, exactly. They looked curious. Some of them were wearing little outfits, almost certainly from Mister Honkers. Danny could see a bunny suit—probably from Easter— and something that looked like a green top hat. They looked like the sort of clothes that an elderly woman with a taste for yard art would put on her stone goose, anyway.

"Do we really want to go into a cave filled with toxic sludge?" asked Wendell.

"We don't *know* it's toxic," said Christiana. "But I wouldn't suggest that we go swimming."

THAT'D BE
AWESOME!

Danny took a few steps forward into the room. Something crunched under his feet.

"Peanut shells," said Christiana, picking one up. "They've been stealing things for a long time."

"Well," said Wendell. "Now what? Do you see my retainer?"

"No," said Danny. "I don't see my granddad's dentures either, and those are practically visible from space."

"Some pack rat middens have multiple chambers," offered Christiana. She pointed. "Can we go up there? I want a better look at that pipe over there."

Since nobody had any better ideas, they walked along the bank of the sludge canal, up to the nearest bridge. It smelled foul, sort of like bleach and car exhaust and farts, rolled into one. Danny wondered if it bothered the pack rats, or if they'd just gotten used to it by now.

The floor rose steeply on the far side of the canal. Danny skidded on what looked like wet cardboard, and his foot hit something hard and angular underneath.

"I think there are old stairs under here," he said.

"There must be," said Wendell, "because I've got a handrail." The iguana clung to the iron railing and peered out over the sludge. "Looks like it's coming out of that pipe. It's a slow ooze, but I think it's still flowing."

"Pack rats didn't build this," said Christiana. "This looks like a sewer or something."

"Not quite," said Danny, who was something of an expert on sewers, after the potato salad incident. "The pipes are a lot bigger in a sewer, just in case everybody flushes all at once."

"That grill looks almost like teeth," said Wendell.

"Maybe the pack rats are obsessed with dentures for a reason," said Danny.

They reached the wall. It was covered in mud and dried algae, but there were square shapes underneath.

Danny scraped muck off the wall with the side of his hand, revealing the edge of a metal sign. "There's something under here, guys!"

"The old hospital!" breathed Wendell.

"So the sludge . . . ?" said Danny.

"Toxic waste, maybe," said Christiana. "Hospitals were a lot nastier back in the old days. They used all kinds of icky chemicals, and they weren't nearly as good about how they threw out radioactive stuff."

"When I get home," said Wendell, gazing into the sludge, "I am going to write a very stern letter to the Environmental Protection Agency . . ."

Danny cleared more mud away, revealing several metal levers and a corroded sign. He squinted at it. It looked like instructions, but he couldn't quite make them out.

He reached for a lever.

IF YOU TOUCH THAT LEVER, DANNY DRAGONBREATH, I WILL CHUCK YOU INTO THE SLIME HEAD-FIRST!

AWWW . . .

"But it might do something neat!"

"It might also cause toxic waste to shoot out of the pipe and drown us!" said Christiana.

Danny considered this. The odds of toxic waste shooting out of the pipe were probably higher than, say, candy bars raining from the ceiling. Still. It was a *lever.* Not pulling it was almost criminal!

He gave it a longing look as they went back down the stairs.

"No sign of my retainer," said Wendell. "We have to keep looking!"

"There's another tunnel," Danny pointed out. "Let's try there."

This tunnel was much larger than the other. Danny suspected that it had once been a corridor in the hospital basement. The remains of old light fixtures hung from the ceiling.

"I see another sign," said Christiana, pointing.

"Huh. You think that's why they want the clothes?" asked Wendell.

"Don't be silly," said Christiana. "Pack rats can't read."

"They could look at the pictures," said Danny. "And it's only a few words to

figure out. Maybe they're taking it as a commandment or something."

He expected Christiana to say something sarcastic, but she only looked at the sign thoughtfully. "Hmmmm . . ."

The tunnel opened into an enormous room with a partially intact concrete floor, although you could only see bits around the edges.

There was a huge mound of sticks and twigs and trash in the center of the room. A hole in the ceiling let in sunlight. All over the cavern, pack rats peered out of holes and over the top of trash, watching them.

"Some pack rat middens are really big," said Christiana slowly, "and have lasted for hundreds of years. But I didn't expect anything like this!"

Danny took a few steps forward. The rats were a lot smaller than he was, and they didn't look hostile . . . but there were more of them than there were of him. If it came to a fight, Christiana could probably take one or two, and Wendell would cover the weeping and cowering, but Danny would have to do most of the work.

He didn't want to breathe fire in here, even if he could do it reliably. The mound of trash was mostly twigs, and it looked *really* flammable. Like stop-drop-and-roll-isn't-going-to-help flammable.

HOW ARE WE GOING TO FIND MY RETAINER IN ALL THIS? THAT MOUND IS HUGE!

"It would be near the top," said Christiana practically. "They aren't going to dig down to the middle of a forty-foot trash heap just to hide your retainer."

"I guess we should go to the top of the heap, then," said Danny.

He kept an eye on the pack rats. They still didn't look aggressive, but they were starting to look worried. He could hear scufflings and rustlings as they moved around the mound, coming closer and closer to the climbers.

"They're coming up behind us too," whispered Christiana.

"Oh *great* . . ." said Wendell.

Danny risked a glance over his shoulder. There were pack rats below them. He could see bright eyes shining in the dim light.

"I think I see something at the top," said Christiana, tilting her head back. "Under the hole in the ceiling."

"Is it my retainer?" asked Wendell hopefully.

"I don't know. Was your retainer three feet tall?"

"If you get the Black Plague, I'm not sending a get-well card."

Danny poked his head over the top of the mound.

THE GREAT GOOSE

"Well," said Christiana. "That's something you don't see every day."

"The Secret Pack Rat Cult of the Stone Lawn Goose," said Wendell. "Of course it is. I don't know why I didn't think of that right off the bat." He began to giggle hysterically, until Danny elbowed him in the ribs and he stopped.

Wendell was not terribly good with stress.

"I think I see your retainer," said Christiana. "And—aha!"

"What about Granddad's dentures?" asked Danny.

"What's Mister Honkers standing on?" asked Wendell.

Danny blinked.

He had expected his grandfather's dentures to be large, of course—Grandfather Turlingsward was a very large reptile!—but a set of dentures large enough for a three-foot-high concrete goose to stand on . . . well, that was something.

"We're going to have to take the top and bottom half out separately," he said. "I mean, I can carry one, and Christiana, if you can carry the other . . ."

"Aren't we getting ahead of ourselves?" asked Wendell, watching the pack rat in the raincoat fuss with the position of the brooch. "I'm not sure they're going to just let us waltz out of here with that stuff. There's . . . kind of a lot of them now."

Wendell was right. More and more were arriving. Squeaking and chittering rang all around the room. Danny didn't like the way their tails were lashing.

"So they're bringing Mister Honkers all these . . . what . . . offerings?" he asked.

"I'm not sure that pack rats are smart enough for that," said Christiana dubiously.

"They're wearing clothes," said Danny. "Probably because the sign told them to! What more do you want?"

"Yeah, but they didn't *make* the clothes. Now, if they had obvious language skills, or signs of tool use . . ."

THEY'RE STARTING TO LOOK ANGRY. THERE MUST BE SOME WAY TO COMMUNICATE WITH THEM.

I COULD TRY TO USE MY AWESOME BUTTERFLY TAMING SKILLS! YOU USE A FIRM VOICE AND A VERY SMALL CHAIR—

OR, Y'KNOW, I COULD TRY TO TALK TO THEM, LIKE I DID THE SEWER RATS.

He turned to the rat in the raincoat and said, "Um—squeak?"

It cocked its head. Another pack rat, slightly lower down the mound, made a noise that sounded a lot like a snicker.

Danny wondered if he had a sewer rat accent or something.

SO, UH, MISTER PACK RAT, I SEE YOU'VE GOT ALL THIS STUFF HERE . . .

"And I realize you think you need it for Mister Honkers, but . . . uh . . . we kinda need it back." He waved at the dentures.

The pack rat appeared to think about this for a minute, then said slowly, "Squeeaak?"

I'M SURE HE CAN TALK *TO* RATS. I JUST QUESTION WHETHER THE RATS UNDERSTAND IT.

"The stuff," said Danny patiently, ignoring the conversation behind him. "We need it back."

"Squeak!" Two pack rats hastily moved to shield their treasures. The rain-slickered pack rat wrung its paws.

"We're not trying to steal it," said Danny. "I mean, you stole it first, but—well, look, that doesn't matter. It's okay. We just need it back. My granddad needs his dentures, and my friend needs his retainer."

"Tell them it's a matter of life and death!" whispered Wendell.

"It's a matter of life and death," Danny repeated.

"Squeak! Squeak-squeeaaaaak!" cried the rat in the raincoat.

"He thinks it's a matter of life and death too," said Danny to his friends. "I think he's afraid that if we take the stuff, Mister Honkers will get angry."

"It's a stone goose," said Christiana. "What's it going to do—fall over on them?"

SQUEAK!

"Oh, I get it," said Danny, nodding. "If Mister Honkers is angry, there won't be any more clothes. They need the clothes. The sign says the clothes protect against the slime. They don't like the slime. They brought him here, but there haven't been any more clothes, so they're trying to make him happy by bringing him stuff. Then . . . sorry, what was that?"

"Squeak squeak squeak!"

THE GREAT GOOSE WILL BRING FORTH CLOTHING FOR THE FAITHFUL AND . . . I DUNNO, SOMETHING ABOUT SMITING.

"Squeak!" said the pack rat, nodding emphatically.

"But there aren't going to be any more clothes now that they've taken it away from Miss Flicktongue!" said Christiana.

"What was that about smiting?" asked Wendell.

"Yeah, but they don't know that."

"Squeak!"

"I'm really concerned about this whole smiting business," said Wendell.

"We have to take the stuff," said Danny to the rats. "I *promise* Mister Honkers won't get angry. Seriously. He's—err—a merciful goose?"

"Squeak!"

"Maybe we should go," said Wendell.

"What? We're in the middle of negotiations here!" Danny said.

"Squeak?"

"Are you saying that the pack rats are actually intelligent?"

I REALLY THINK WE SHOULD GO.

"Now would be a *really good time* to get out of here . . ."

Danny opened his mouth to ask Wendell what his problem was, and then he noticed that Wendell's retainer wasn't on the platform anymore.

Unfortunately, the pack rats noticed it at the same time.

"Wendell!" cried Danny, not sure if he was mad or astonished that Wendell had had the nerve to steal his own retainer back.

"Well, I couldn't leave it!" said Wendell, clutching the bit of dental equipment to his chest.

MOM WOULD FREAK OUT! AND WHEN SHE FREAKS OUT, SHE COOKS!

The pack rats were not pleased. Suddenly they looked very hostile indeed.

"I don't think they're happy, Wendell!"

"I couldn't leave it here and let them get plague all over it!"

Several of them picked up sticks. The ends were pointed, and looked a great deal like spears.

"Hey, look!" said Christiana, delighted. "Signs of tool use!"

"Squeak!" yelled the rat in the raincoat. "Squeak, squeak SQUEAK!"

"I could really use a little tiny chair about now," said Wendell wretchedly.

"Stop!" yelled Danny. "We can talk about this!"

"It's not that I want to be stabbed to death by intelligent pack rats," said Christiana, "but you have to admit, if you're gonna go, it's much more interesting to be killed by a tool-using species that may have attained sentience—"

"I don't have to admit anything!" yelled Wendell.

"Sacrifices are common fixtures of many primitive cults," said Christiana thoughtfully. "I wonder if they're planning on sacrificing us to Mister Honkers."

I AM NOT GOING TO BE SACRIFICED TO A STONE LAWN GOOSE!

"We may not have a choice!" said Danny, backing away from a spear-carrying pack rat. He didn't dare breathe fire—if the mound of trash caught, they'd burn to death before the pack rats managed to stab them.

"Squeak! Squeak-squeak!" The rat in the raincoat had lost its temper and was screaming at the other pack rats in a frenzy.

Danny tried desperately to think of something—anything!—that would appease the furious rodents.

He felt something cool against his back. The plastic edge of Grandfather Turlingsward's giant dentures dug into his shoulder.

"SQUEAK!" The rat raised a tiny fist.

"I'm too smart to die!" cried Wendell. "I've never even taken the SATs!"

Danny, in desperation, jumped on top of the enormous dentures and lunged for Mister Honkers.

The pack rats let out squeaking gasps and pulled back. Danny shoved at the goose, and it rocked on its base. If he had to, he was sure that he could push it over and maybe smash it against the pile of offerings below.

"Squeak!" cried the rat in the raincoat. "Squeaaak!?"

"They're backing off!" said Wendell hopefully.

"Yeah, but now what?" asked Christiana. "We can't carry that thing all the way back to the surface—once we're in the tunnel, they can get us from behind!"

Danny thought even this was overly optimistic. As soon as Mister Honkers was off the mound, and in no danger of smashing, the pack rats would be all over them.

It was a standoff. Both sides were stuck. The rats couldn't move, and Danny and his friends couldn't get away.

"How are we going to convince them to give up our stuff?" asked Wendell.

"I'd be happy with not being skewered, myself," said Christiana.

I HAVE TO SCRUB MY RETAINER TO GET PACK RAT GERMS OFF IT! MY TEETH COULD BE MOVING OUT OF ALIGNMENT AS WE SPEAK!

"I'll think of something!" said Danny desperately. Chasing his grandfather's dentures had gotten them into this mess, and if Wendell was killed by pack rats, he'd never forgive himself. (He'd probably feel a little bad about Christiana too.)

The rats moved restlessly. More of them seemed to be appearing in the cavern all the time.

Christiana cleared her throat. "Say, Danny . . ."

"Yes?"

"What if we got Miss Flicktongue to make them their own clothes?"

A HARD BARGAIN

"Okay," said Danny, leaning back. "So you let us go, *with* the dentures."

"Squeak."

"And the retainer."

"Squeak."

"In return, we give you two shirts, one jacket—"

"My mother is going to ask where my shirt went," muttered Wendell.

"Tell her you lost it heroically defending your retainer," muttered Christiana.

"In return for that," said Danny, ignoring this,

"in addition to the shirts, we will introduce you to Miss Flicktongue—"

"Squeak?"

"The Bride of the Great Goose. The one who makes the clothes."

"Can we trust them?" whispered Wendell.

Danny snorted. "He just asked the same thing about you. After all, you stole his offering to Mister Honkers. Which reminds me, they want to hold on to your retainer until we've handled the sludge."

"What? No!"

"C'mon, Wendell . . ."

Wendell folded his arms and pointedly ignored the dragon.

"You have to let the rats hold it while we fix the problem. Otherwise they think we'll run out on the bargain."

Wendell muttered something and fished his retainer out of his pocket. "Fine. But don't let them do anything weird to it."

"I'm more worried about keeping our end of the bargain," said Christiana. "Those pipe mechanisms are really old. What if they don't work?"

"Then you'd better figure out a way to make a toxic waste containment unit out of peanut shells and miniature Santa suits," said Danny.

Christiana and Wendell screwed up their faces in identical expressions of deep thought.

"I'm gonna need some rubber bands," said Wendell finally. "Or a bungee cord."

"Let's just hope the mechanisms work."

The pack rat leader seemed pleased with their bargain. Danny stuck out a hand. The pack rat sniffed and then shook it.

"Now," said Danny. "Let's go see about this toxic ooze . . ."

The trio of kids and a phalanx of pack rats marched back to the sludge-filled chamber. The pack rats had brought their spears. Danny hoped that he'd gotten the *trying*-to-fix part across in his negotiations.

The rats clustered around the base of the steps, while Danny, Wendell, and Christiana climbed to the platform alone.

"Okay," said Wendell, studying the levers. "I *think* this is the outflow from an old storage tank under the hospital. There should be a manual switch to shut off the pipe."

"Won't the tank explode or something?" asked Danny, having a vision of a geyser of toxic sludge transforming Sunny Acres into Slimy Acres. Normally he would have thought this was awesome, but he had a gloomy feeling that he'd be the one who had to clean it up. Danny Dragonbreath *hated* cleaning.

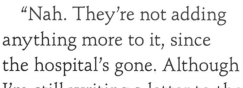

GET SCRUBBING, MISTER!

"Nah. They're not adding anything more to it, since the hospital's gone. Although I'm still writing a letter to the EPA."

"Our bigger problem is whether the mechanisms have rusted too badly," said Christiana. She squinted at the sign. "I think it's this switch, then that one, then pull that lever there all the way to the bottom . . ."

Wendell nodded. He pushed one of the switches. Grinding noises started inside the walls, and the pack rats drew together, squeaking worriedly.

Christiana threw the second switch. The grinding noises got louder, combined with the squeal of abused metal. The wall shook. Bits of dirt filtered down from the ceiling.

Danny grabbed the heavy metal lever in both hands and heaved. It stuck fast. Danny threw his full weight against it, gritting his teeth—and the metal snapped off in his hand.

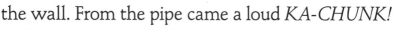

UH, WAS IT SUPPOSED TO DO THIS?

"Aaaaaand we're doomed," said Wendell.

More grindings and rattlings started inside the wall. From the pipe came a loud *KA-CHUNK!*

"Is it working?" asked Danny.

KA-CHUNK!

"Squeak?" called the pack rat leader.

KA-CHUNK!

"I think something's stuck," said Christiana. "The pipe's trying to close, but there's something in the way."

KA-CHUNK!

"If it keeps doing this, the ceiling's going to come down," said Wendell.

"Do something!" said Danny. "Flip another lever!"

"There's only the one lever! You're holding it!"

The pack rats were milling around the base of the stairs, squeaking nervously. Danny did not think that his bargain would hold if he accidentally destroyed their home.

"If somebody gets into the pipe, maybe we can knock out the bar!" said Wendell. "It's probably in even worse shape than the lever."

"Won't they have to stand in toxic sludge?" asked Christiana. "And by 'they,' I of course mean 'Danny.'"

"Well, obviously," said Danny, who had no illusions about his role in the group.

"Not if he hangs off the railing," said Wendell. "If we grab his tail, I think he can reach the bar."

One of the bridges collapsed behind them. The ooze engulfed it. Several pack rats rushed to rescue their fellows from falling masonry.

"We don't have much time!" said Danny, climbing onto the railing. "I think the dens are going to fall down next, and there might be baby pack rats or something in there!"

"Actually, baby pack rats are called pups," said Wendell.

"That's not helpful, Wendell!" Danny ducked his head under the railing. Christiana grabbed his tail and braced herself.

"Can you reach the pipe?"

Up close, the grill over the pipe looked even more like teeth—big pointy teeth that were trying to chew their way through something. They went up and down, striking against a heavy bar across the opening. Every time they hit, they bounced back up with a loud *KA-CHUNK!*

The bar wobbled every time the grill hit it. Danny thought it would probably break eventually no matter what—but not before the cavern

roof fell down on them. He banged it experimentally with his fist. It felt distressingly solid.

"I need a rock!" he yelled. "Something!"

Wendell looked around wildly. In a huge underground room full of junk, there ought to be plenty of rocks, right? Why couldn't he see one?

KA-CHUNK!

KA-CHUNK!

A den collapsed. Several pack rats climbed out of it, shaking themselves off and squeaking in terror.

"Now might not be the best time to mention it," said Christiana conversationally, "but my arms are getting tired."

"If you drop me into the toxic sludge, I'll— I'll—" Danny was unable to come up with a threat dire enough. "I'll call you Brainiac until the whole school picks up on it!"

"Pfff!" said Christiana. "Free advertising."

KA-CHUNK!

"Squeak?" The pack rat leader climbed over the

edge of the railing. In its paws it carried a round metal object.

"What?" Danny took the object from the rat. It looked almost like a miniature iron cauldron . . . in fact, it looked exactly like the sort of miniature iron cauldron that an elderly lizard might put out in front of her beloved stone lawn goose on Halloween, probably combined with a witch's hat and miniature broom.

Thank goodness for Miss Flicktongue.

"Perfect!" said Danny. He swung the cauldron at the bar. It went *BONNNNG!*

Had the bar given a little? He swung again.

"You're slipping!" said Christiana. Wendell grabbed for Danny's tail. The pack rat climbed over him to the railing, and Danny felt tiny paws on his left foot.

BONNNNNG! This time the bar was definitely bent. When the grill hit it, instead of *KA-CHUNK,* it went *KA-CHUNGA-CHUNGA-CHUNK!* and the pipe shook so violently that Wendell lost hold of Danny's tail.

Danny figured one more blow ought to knock the rusted bar clean off the wall. It would also probably knock him clean off the railing and into the ooze.

He heard the squeak of terrified pack rats as another den collapsed. Really, what choice was there?

The bar broke. Christiana lost her hold. Danny slid over the railing, teetered sickeningly on the edge—and a dozen tiny paws clutched at him and held on tight.

The grill slammed down. As Danny dangled, the river of ooze beneath him slowed, stopped, and began to dwindle away.

SWEET REWARDS

"I thought Miss Flicktongue was very nice about the whole thing," said Christiana an hour later, lugging the bottom half of Grandfather Turlingsward's dentures through the grass.

"Yeth," said Wendell, who had scrubbed his retainer for five minutes before pronouncing it free of Black Plague. "I mean, we did get her denthureth back, but the ratth . . ."

"Well, they're kinda cute," said Danny. "Once she got over them wearing clothes at all . . . I mean, you *know* she's going to dress them in little pink smocks and thingies, but I guess they won't mind."

"Good thing she still had all those extra outfits for Mister Honkers."

"I thought the little panda thuit wath pretty cute," said Wendell.

"Yeah . . ." Danny rubbed the back of his neck. "I still say there's something *weird* about a pack rat in a bikini, though . . ."

"And a goose in a bikini *isn't* weird?" asked Christiana.

Danny shuddered. He'd been trying not to think about it.

"And you have to admit, she didn't even blink at being called . . . what was it?"

"The Bride of the Great Goose," said Danny, grinning. The pack rats had been *very* impressed to learn that Miss Flicktongue was the source of Mister Honkers's finery.

"Not that they *need* the clothes," said Christiana. "I mean, we shut off the sludge overflow, and the bikini couldn't have been much use anyway."

"Yeah, but they like the clothes," said Danny. "And if it makes them happy . . ."

"I jutht with they hadn't claimed my thirt," said Wendell sadly. "Mom ith gonna be mad. Not ath mad ath if I lotht my retainer, mind you." He shuddered. "And that wath too clothe for comfort. I thought that one wathn't going to give it back."

Danny shook his head.

After they'd shut off the sludge pipe, he'd thought they were home free—until they tried to get Wendell's retainer back and discovered a very small pack rat wearing it as a hat.

Fortunately the pack rat leader had come to their rescue, and Danny had calmed Wendell down.

"Squeak!"

"Oh god! Pack rat cooties!"

"Squeeeak . . ."

"Now, Wendell . . ."

The pack rat leader had exchanged a look with Danny. It was a *why do we put up with this?* look. Danny really felt they'd bonded.

They came around the corner of Miss Flicktongue's house and found her sitting on her front step with a measuring tape and one of the pack rats. It was staring up at her adoringly while she noted down its dimensions.

"Hey, Granddad!" called Danny. "We got your dentures!"

Grandfather Turlingsward was lying on his rock and glaring at the pack rats. He lifted his head as Danny approached.

"Well. Well, well, well."

Grandfather Turlingsward took the dentures, turned them over a few times, and said, "Well . . . they *look* like mine . . ."

"I'm pretty sure they're yours, Granddad," said Danny wearily. He really wanted to go home. It was getting late, and he wanted dinner. He might even go to bed early, which generally required divine intervention. It had been a *very* long day. Negotiating a truce with a group of clothes-obsessed pack rats really took it out of you.

"And did you bring back my brooch?" demanded Grandfather Turlingsward.

Wendell stepped forward with the brooch. Grandfather Turlingsward snatched it up and eyed it suspiciously.

"Well," he said again. "Hmm. I suppose that it didn't take any harm. You're sure it was pack rats?"

"Completely sure," said Danny. He was a bit annoyed. He hadn't expected serious praise, but would it kill his grandfather to say thanks?

"I still think *she* had something to do with it,"

said Grandfather Turlingsward, glaring across the street.

Danny sighed. He'd had enough. The pack rats wouldn't steal any more dentures—at least, as long as Miss Flicktongue kept making them little outfits—and he was tired.

"Oh, no!" said Christiana. "My slime molds have probably run the maze twice by now, and I wasn't there to give them a treat!" She took off at a run toward the bus stop. Wendell jogged after her.

As they hurried away, Danny heard an enormous throat clear behind him, and Grandfather Turlingsward said, "Wait up, Danny."

Danny blinked. He wasn't sure that he'd ever heard his granddad actually use his name.

YOU—ERR—
YOU DID GOOD.
GETTING MY DENTURES
BACK. THAT WAS
GOOD WORK.

"Really?" asked Danny. He didn't have any-thing in his hoard half as good—a tenth as good!—as the brooch. "Seriously?"

"A young dragon needs a nice piece for his hoard," said Grandfather Turlingsward. "Gives you a good start. Don't go trading it for baseball cards, now."

Danny, who mostly knew about baseball cards as a historical curiosity, clutched the brooch to his chest.

I WON'T.
I WON'T TRADE IT EVER.
THANKS, GRANDDAD.

"Hmmph!" muttered Grandfather Turlingsward. "You young people today . . . I don't know. Now get off my lawn!"

AND THE WINNER OF THE DRAGONBREATH CREATE-YOUR-OWN-COMIC CONTEST IS . . .

KRISTIN CAMPBELL,

AGE 13, FOR HER AWESOME "SECRET AGENT WENDELL" COMIC!

HONORABLE MENTIONS GO TO SAMANTHA WUEHLER, AGE 12, AND SAGE UHL, AGE 13.

CONGRATULATIONS, KRISTIN, SAMANTHA, AND SAGE, AND THANKS TO EVERYONE WHO ENTERED!

KRISTIN RECEIVED A FULL, SIGNED SET OF THE DRAGONBREATH BOOKS, AND DANNY WANTS TO GIVE EVERYONE A HIGH FIVE!